I0517109

BOUND BY INSIGHT

FLAMES OF LIGHT

A PREQUEL

Katrina A. Bauer

Copyright © 2022 by Katrina A. Bauer
All rights reserved.

No part of this book may be used or reproduced in any manner whatsoever without written permission from the author, except in the case of brief quotations used
for review purposes.

This is a work of fiction. Names, characters, places, and incidents are solely the product of the author's imagination and/or are used fictitiously. Any resemblance to actual persons, living or dead, organization, actual events, or locales is entirely coincidental.

Editor:
Sherrie Coutu

Cover Design:
Kate T Sib

Book Formatting:
Joe Dugdale (www.joe.ma)

DISCLAIMER

The stories in this book are intended for mature, adult audiences only. All characters in this work are 18 years of age or older and participate in consensual sex.

DEDICATION

To my cousin Lauren, without your endless understanding and support, I could not have found my well of joy in writing again. You are one of the strongest women and mothers I know. From the bottom of my heart, I am eternally grateful for everything you have done for me.

ACKNOWLEDGMENT

This book would never have come to be without the guidance of Lia Violet and her encouragement in trying my hand at writing in the Paranormal world she and Ginger Leone created.

I am so grateful for the support of my husband and our four princesses for always being in my corner and helping me follow my dreams.

To my marvelous editor, Sherrie Coutu, thank you for making this story shimmer and glow. To my insanely talented cover artist Kate, thank you for giving my story vision a unique and hot look.

My amazing assistant Sylv Kerslake, thank you for your patience and hard work. Your skills and creativity shine like the sun. You have brought me into your light.

Joe Dugdale, the way you formatted my book was better than I could have ever imagined! Thank you.

CONTENTS

CHAPTER 1

Artemis Meagher stood on the balcony of their fifteenth home in the last twenty-eight years. She glanced down to the garden sanctuary her husband, Belenos, duplicated after each move. A smile curved her lips at how Belenos remembered the length of the willow branches over the lake. Even the white benches twinkled at the edge of the water. Every time he recreates the garden for their girls, he brings something from their first meeting in her enchanted garden. Her mind formed a memory from when their daughters were young after their nightly prayers.

"Brigid, take Demeter and Cassandra by the hand," she said as her children came together. Belenos picked up Aradia as she giggled and rested her head on her father's shoulder. He came up beside her and laced their fingers together. "Ladies, go right in and brush your teeth."

"Yes, Mama," they answered in unison.

"Then it's storytime?" Aradia brought her head up, looking expectantly at her mother.

She caressed her youngest's cheek. "Yes, little one."

Once all of their little ones were snug in their beds, she sat on the one with her older daughters Brigid and Demeter. Belenos sat across from her on the other bed with their youngest daughters, Cassandra and Aradia.

Aradia snuggled next to her father as he ran his fingers down Cassandra's arm next to them.

"Mama, can you tell us the story of the Princess and the Prince?" Brigid asked, curling up on her side with her bird stuffed animal.

"The Princess and her Consort," Demeter corrected. "Right, Mama?"

"Yes, it is, but I think Prince is also correct."

Brigid gave her sister a smug smile.

"Mama, can you start the story," Cassandra murmured, holding her teddy bear tight to her chest.

"Alright." She smiled down at her daughters. "Once upon a time, there was a princess."

"A beautiful princess with long red hair," her husband added.

She sighed. "A beautiful princess walked in an enchanted garden after her nightly prayers when she noticed a gentleman sitting on a bench overlooking the small pond."

"Was he a handsome gentleman?" Brigid asked.

"Oh, yes."

His onyx hair shimmered in the moonlight as he stared out over the water. The princess wondered why he sat all alone and went over to ask him. But, the moment she got close, he turned to her. His eyes were like two sapphires, and they took her breath away until the princess saw the distress in them. "How did you get in?" she asked.

"I was walking, and my steps led me here."

She glanced down at his worn shoes, and the shirt he had on seemed too big for him. So she questioned, "Were you walking in the forest?"

"Yes. I went to my uncle's cabin and didn't sense his magic. I worried he could be in some trouble. So I started searching for him."

"Who is your uncle?"

"Sir Benigno, but I called him Big Ben."

Her heart sank as she lowered to sit next to him on the bench. "Sir Ben was my parents' groundkeeper and friend."

A small smile graced his lips. "I can recognize some of his touches." He turned to her. "Was? What?"

"I'm sorry, Sir Ben passed away last week."

His eyes twinkled with tears. "I am too late. I came to tell him his sister, my mother, died."

She reached for his hand to offer him comfort. The moment their skin touched, sparks tingled up her arm.

"And his too," her husband added.

Heat went to her cheeks as she continued.

"You must be Sir Ben's nephew he talked so much about?"

"He talked about me?" The hopefulness in his voice made her want to stay.

"Yes, he said you are unique and have a way with herbs and would be a great man one day."

His head fell and went side to side. "I'm not half the man he was. He made the grounds change with his magic of the earth. I only know how to mix the things he grew."

"Sir Ben believed in you too, so you must be an extraordinary person."

"Not extraordinary enough to save my mother, and as it turns out, my uncle." A tear slipped past his long lashes.

"I am sorry for your loss." She let him lace their fingers as something shifted inside her.

"Like two puzzle pieces fitting together," Belenos added with a sly curve of his lips.

"Yes, plus the princess had never been touched by anyone."

Brigid raised her head. "Why did no one touch the princess?"

Artemis brushed back her daughter's hair. "The

princess had the power to read people's minds when they touched her. Except for the man whose hand the princess held."

"Is that how the princess knew they belonged together?" Demeter yawned.

"Yes, in a way, not being able to read him gave the princess a freedom she never experienced before, and the prince intrigued her."

Demeter asked, "When did the guards come?"

"Before the prince had a chance to kiss the princess."

"The guards always had impeccable timing," her husband sighed under his breath.

She continued with a shake of her head at Belenos.

The palace guards pulled them apart, yelling the prince was trying to kidnap the princess. Voices crashed into the princess's mind all at once, and she stumbled. The prince fought the guards hold on him and shouted to unhand the princess because he noticed how their touch affected her. They listened to the prince's command and let go of the princess.

Once the princess's mind cleared of all the voices, and she could stand, the princess commanded the guards to release Sir Benigno's nephew. One of the guards spoke. "Sorry, Princess, we need to bring him on the order of the queen."

The princess ran to the one who spoke. "Please, Fadias, let him go."

He shook his head at the princess. "Take him to the queen. I will escort the princess." Fadias motioned everyone ahead of them then asked the princess, "Did he touch you?"

The princess stood in front of the guard to stop him. "I touched him to offer comfort since the poor man lost his mother and uncle in less than a week."

The guard narrowed his eyes at the princess. "Did you read him? Can he be trusted?"

"No, I cannot read him. Sir Benigno trusted him," the princess answered as Fadias began to walk again. They entered the throne room, a place the princess knew the queen did not like. The queen, with her long red hair and emerald gown, entered from the side door, followed by her tall, dark-haired consort. The prince fought against the guards, trying to see the princess. He went to his knees as the queen stepped in front of him. The queen frowned down at the guards, and they knelt *quickly next to the prince. The princess smirked when Fadias joined them.*

"My queen," the prince started. "I apologize if I offended the princess. My name is Belenos Meagher, Sir Benigno's nephew, and I am at your service, my queen." The prince bowed his head respectfully.

Then Fadias made his way over to the queen and whispered in her ear.

"Was he telling the queen that the princess could touch the prince?" Demeter asked with a yawn.

"Yes, he was."

"Tattletale," Brigid added.

"My thoughts exactly," her husband piped in.

Artemis inhaled with a shake of her head. "All the queen said was 'interesting,' then told the guards to release the prince, and they were dismissed."

"Did the tattletale go too, Mama?" Cassandra yawned.

"Yes..."

Then the queen motioned for the prince and princess to follow her. The prince remained on his knees. The princess rushed to his side to help the prince up, but he shook his head and remained kneeling. Finally, the queen said, "You may rise, sir."

The prince raised his head. "My queen, I am not a knight, just a common man."

Then the queen did the most fantastic thing. She turned to her consort, who wore a beautiful sword at his side, and held out her hand. The consort gently handed it to the queen, and she said, "I can correct one of your issues." The queen placed the sword on one of the prince's shoulders than the other and said, "You may rise, Sir Belenos Meagher, and there is nothing common about you. Princess, please bring your mate with you." The princess took the new knight by the hand, and they followed the queen and her consort into a room filled with soft couches and chairs. The queen sat in a very cushioned chair the color of the sun. Her consort stood to her right. The queen motioned them to sit on the loveseat across from her. She laced her fingers with her consort as he perched on the arm of her chair.

"The princess blushed so prettily as their sides touched," her husband added.

"Why?" Brigid yawned.

Artemis's cheeks heated as her husband chuckled. "Because the prince was warm, and his touch made her tingle." She held Belenos's gaze and whispered, "It still does."

The queen studied them both then said, "I have had a vision of this man for years coming for you, Princess. He is your protector and mate."

The princess looked at the queen. "Mate?"

The consort brought their joined hands to his lips and kissed the queen's fingers. "Princess, this is the man the fates have found for you to be your lifelong partner," the queen continued in a more serious tone. "I have also seen many dangers for the two of you. So if you do not want to face them together, then I suggest you separate because the longer you stay together, it will be harder to keep you both apart."

The princess turned to the prince and, at that moment, knew she wanted to be together forever.

"The prince would give his life for the princess always." Her husband smiled over at her.

"How romantic," Cassandra sighed.

Her husband bent down and kissed their daughter on the forehead. "Yes, it is."

"What were the dangers, Mama?" Demeter piped up. Their second child always wanted to know every aspect of a situation.

"Being the queen, there is always a danger of some bad people who want to take her throne. Since the princess had a gift of being able to read people's thoughts, it made her especially valuable." She paused, not wanting to alarm her children.

Thankfully her husband continued, "One of the dangers was since the princess could not read the prince, he could be used to lead the bad people to the princess and the queen."

"Papa, what did they do?" the girls asked in unison.

"The prince got down on one knee and asked the princess to marry him. He pledged his life to her and said he would always protect the princess. So they were married that night in a private service with just the princess's parents, the queen and her consort, and the tattletale."

Artemis shook her head as their daughters giggled. "They traveled the world seeking adventure and helping the communities they stayed in." She smiled down at her children. "Now it is time to sleep, my darlings." She kissed each of her daughters on the forehead before her husband followed her. "Good night, our blessed daughters of the Goddesses."

"Good night, Mama and Papa." They all yawned, snuggling into their beds.

CHAPTER 2

The memory faded as the cool May breeze blew the silk of her nightgown at her ankles. Belenos came up behind her and wrapped his arms around Artemis's waist. "Where are you, my love?" he asked.

She leaned back against her husband and rested her head on his shoulder. "Thinking back to when our daughters were little, we told them the fairytale about us."

"Our life has been a fairytale. Yet, we did as we promised to travel the world and give our daughters an exciting but normal life."

"Has it been exciting and normal to always look over our shoulders and wait for the next shoe to drop?" Then, turning in Belenos's arms, she linked her hands behind his head.

He leaned down, captured his wife's lips, and then trailed kisses down her neck. "It has been an adventure."

Artemis quivered as the familiar rush of heat went through her body. She let herself enjoy the moment of being caged by her prince. "You cannot keep trying to distract me with your kisses." She pulled back as his mouth hovered over hers.

"Is it working, my dear?" he asked, nibbling her jaw.

"Yes." Her head fell back to give him better access to her collarbone. She weaved her fingers through his hair as he placed open mouth kisses down her chest. She gave a tug before he got too far. Within a second, his lips covered hers as he commandeered her mouth. A moan vibrated through him as he scooped her up.

Her white gown flowed around them. "Let us put our worries away for tonight. I want to worship my princess with my body."

She nestled her head under his chin. "I do love the way you worship me." She chuckled, reaching for the top button of his blue oxford. He lowered her down onto their bed. "Afterwards, my prince, we need to talk about our next move."

"Of course." He stood to take in the sight of her lying back with open arms to welcome him. He covered her with his body and rested his forearms on either side of her head. "If I do my job at pleasing my princess right, we won't be able to talk until morning."

"We'll see." She gave him a sly smirk.

"Challenge accepted, my princess." His finger traced the ribbon at the base of her throat. "Someone is wearing way too many clothes."

"Yes, you are." She reached for his buttons again. "I do enjoy undressing you slowly." Artemis got his shirt open and ran her fingers up his warm chest, enjoying how his muscles jumped under her caress. She took a moment to trace the tattoo of the tree of life with tiny sparkly leaves over his heart that matched hers.

"Mmm," he murmured. Then, with a snap of his fingers, Artemis's clothes disappeared. "Now, this is more my speed." He brought his mouth down to her shoulder, kissing a path to her breasts.

"The reveal is half the fun." She moaned as his lips closed on her nipple, sending a wave of pleasure through her body. Then, with a snap of her fingers, his clothes came off. When their naked bodies touched, she was ignited with a fire deep in her belly.

"My prince, I need you." She ran her hand down his back to his sculpted butt cheeks and held him closer.

Belenos paid homage to her other breast as she begged, "Please, my prince."

"As you wish, my princess." He covered her lips with his as his tongue entered her mouth. Then, he lifted her thighs around his waist and penetrated her with one great thrust. "I love you."

He curled his arms around her shoulders to bring her up against his chest. She felt the rapid beat of his heart and the tingle of their tattoos as their bodies joined and raced to completion. "I love you too, my prince!" Artemis cried out as her release peaked.

"You are my life, my princess," Belenos called out and thrust into her one last time.

As they caught their breath, she caressed his back, enjoying the weight of his body. "I still can't believe, after all these years, our mating tattoos still glow as bright as they did the first time we mated."

"It's because we make mad passionate love," he chuckled and rolled them over, still joined.

Artemis settled on his chest, resting her head on her laced fingers so she could hold his stare. "Of course, mad passionate love does last a bit longer." She giggled as he pinched her waist.

His fingers caressed down her back as their bodies cooled. "Well, my beautiful wife, we can take our time now." With a flick of his wrist, the multi-colored quilt from the chair covered them.

"Yes, we can." She ran her palms up his chest until her fingers twirled in the hair at the nape of his neck. Molding her lips to his, desire flared where their bodies still connected. "Are you up for round two?" He rolled on top of her in one fluid motion as he thrust deep inside, fanning their cooling bodies into heated flames of passion.

"Yes!" he gasped and turned their kiss into an all-consuming one.

A squawk of a bird echoed in the room.

"Damn, why didn't I close the doors," Belenos growled and snapped his fingers. "I swear to the Goddess that tattletale has the worst timing." Their clothes reappeared as Belenos flopped on the bed next to her.

Artemis made sure her gown was tied. "You know he only comes if it's important."

They sat up as the bird turned into a man with black as night hair with a cloak of many colors. "I am sorry, Your Royal Highness, for interrupting."

"Are you really, Fadias?" Belenos asked, straightening his clothes.

"Your Royal Highness," Fadias continued as if Belenos never spoke. "Queen Diana has sent me with an urgent message."

Dread washed over Artemis as she scrambled to her feet, and Belenos came to her side. "Has something happened to my mother and father?" She leaned into Belenos's hold.

"The guards of the Jonquil Coven have been infiltrated. Queen Diana and her consort Uilliam do not know who to trust. When I left, they were rotating rooms and enchantments every hour."

She pulled away from her husband, heading for their closet. "I must go to them."

"Wait, I am coming with you." Belenos followed her.

"No, someone needs to stay with the girls."

"Then you stay, and I will go."

"If the guards have been compromised, then killing you would surely bring me back." She grabbed a small bag from a hook inside the closet door. She whispered and waved her hand over it: "Store infinite." She began pulling clothes and items, placing them over the bag, and they disappeared inside the opening.

Belenos took out his wand, waving it over the bag as the items came back out, and he replaced them with his clothes.

"Stop it, my prince." Artemis placed her hands over his. "You have to protect our girls, please."

He pulled her into his chest, caging her in his arms. "I have sworn to protect you, my love. I cannot lose you."

"I can't lose you," she cried, fisting her hands and hitting his chest.

"Mother, I can keep my sisters safe," Brigid whispered from the door as Fadias turned back into a raven and perched on the birdcage in the corner.

Artemis clutched Belenos's shirt as they turned to their oldest. "Darling, your father is staying."

He held her wrist. "No! I am coming with you." He motioned with his head for Brigid to come into the room. "Close the door. Are you the only one up?"

She did as her father asked, walking towards them by the closet. "My sisters are sleeping. I heard a bird squawking. Mother, I can watch over my sisters. We will stay here at the shop, I promise."

Belenos lowered to hold her stare. "Darling, think about it. We can place enchantments on the shop and the apartment above," he spoke softly in her ear.

"Brigid, there is a lot you do not know about us." Artemis pulled away from her husband.

"Mother, I am guessing you have magical powers too." She pointed to the bag hovering in the air and clothes disappearing into it.

With a snap, the bag fell to the ground. "Well, yes. You all have magical powers. We are sorry, sweetheart. We wanted you all to have a normal life. I wish I could stay and explain everything, but your grandparents need me right now." Artemis went to her daughter and sat on the bed. Belenos hovered, crossing his arms over his chest, and shook his head. "Brigid, if you do not think you can do this, we can stay."

"Mother, I have known for a while that I have powers. We all have. We will be fine, and I will explain everything to my sisters. But, please, both of you, go help Grandma and Grandpa."

She hugged her daughter tight. "Brigid, I am so proud of you. Go with your father as he secures our building."

Artemis watched as her daughter and husband left. "Fadias, can you keep them safe?" she asked, rushing to the closet to pack her and her husband's clothes.

The raven turned back into his human form. "Yes, Your Royal Highness."

"They cannot know. I need someone to keep

watch on those Cathain boys. Something is odd about the younger one, and the older one is very conflicted. Belenos is concerned they have some kind of plan."

"I will arrange guards immediately." Fadias turned back into a bird and flew out the window.

"Mother," Brigid called from the door a few moments later, "how will we communicate with you while you're gone?"

Artemis rushed over and pulled her daughter into her arms. "We will send word when it is safe." They sat on the edge of the bed. "Brigid, your grandparents..."

"Have powers too. We know, and the last time they visited, they told us a story about people in a small town with the ability to change into different animals and such."

"What?"

Brigid grimaced. "That was our secret. Please don't tell them I told you."

"I won't. I am guessing you know the town is not just a story." She brushed a lock of red hair out of Brigid's eyes. "You have a special gift of visualizing words and committing them to memory."

"I know. I have other gifts too. Grandma showed me how to move water and fire."

Artemis let out a big sigh. "Really, what else did my sainted mother show you?" she asked, working up a long lecture to give her parents when she saw them.

"Well, not just me exactly." Brigid focused on her lap as she spoke. "Grandma helped Demeter with crystals and Cassandra with her ability with her visions. Grandpa showed Aradia how to heal and explained the danger in Aradia using her powers."

"Oh." Artemis rubbed her forehead as if she had a headache. "It seems your grandparents did not share in our wishes to wait until Aradia turned twenty-five to explain all of this to you."

"Grandma said we needed to learn a few things so we understood our powers and their importance."

Artemis remembered that understanding her skill kept her isolated and very lonely as a child, so she wanted her children to focus on being children.

"What skills do you and Dad have?"

The question drew her back. "I can read people's thoughts if I touch them, your father is gifted in herbs, and we both are gifted in spells."

"Do you get the spells from the books you keep behind the panel in the library?"

With a shake of her head, she asked, "And how do you all know about the library?"

"We did play hide and seek as children."

"Is there anything else you know that I don't?" Artemis kept her hands on her lap, kicking herself for muting her powers with their children.

"Well," she glanced down at her mother's clasped hands. "Grandma and Grandpa did take us to get our wands." Brigid let out an exhausted breath. "We have all been dying to show you." Finally, she whispers, "Reveil," and held out an ornately etched wand to her mother. "It's made from an alder tree and has a core of hair from a mermaid and earth vampire couple freely given. The wandmaker forged this wand under the Alder moon by a lake in Ireland and the mountains of Scotland over two hundred years ago. But, he said, the wand has been waiting for me."

"I know I am going to regret asking this. How long have you and your sisters had wands?"

"Since our grandparents came to visit last summer. They showed us how to use them and a few concealment charms when practicing in the garden. So we do know the packing one too." She pointed to the closet as clothes kept going into the small bag.

"Wow, I guess it was my daughters who have been helping my garden along." Belenos walked over and sat next to their daughter, holding his hand out for the wand. He examined it. "Very nice. This is a very powerful wand, my child. It can help with harnessing your powers to move water and fire. So whose wand is enriching my soil?"

"Demeter's, her wand has the earth crystals and is made from an elder tree under the elder moon," Brigid whispered.

"Sweetheart, you can tell us anything. We are not going to be mad." He glanced over at his wife. "You all have amazing gifts, and we are glad your grandparents had the initiative to show you."

Brigid leaned against Artemis and held her father's hand, and she knew they were in for a long talk. They did not have time for one, but they needed to know their daughters would be safe. She wanted to strangle her parents and hug them at the same time. So instead, Brigid told them about Cassandra's wand being made from a hazel branch and Aradia's from an oak tree.

"We are old enough now to take care of ourselves. I promise I can watch over my sisters."

"What about Cathain boys?" her husband asked with concern.

Their daughter stared down at her fingers as she flexed them. "The shop will be closed, and we won't be leaving, so I think it will be okay. Plus, I broke up with Erebos. He knows I don't feel the same way he feels for me."

"Maybe I should stay." Belenos glanced over Brigid's head.

"No!" Brigid stood and faced them. "I can do this. Grandma said I am more powerful than I know. Erebos might think I'm unique, and that's why he likes me. So we will all call our professors in the morning and explain we have a family emergency and stay in the house." She flicked her wand towards the closet and reversed the spell to have her father's clothes go back in the bag. "Cassandra will warn us if anything changes. We will send you a note with Merlin if we need you." All their eyes focused on the bluebird sleeping in his cage. "Now, both of you go."

If it was not for her daughter's determination and conviction, Artemis might suggest Belenos stay. "Don't leave the house, please." She let the beg play in her voice. At the same time, she held her daughter and lowered her guards as she read how Brigid planned on protecting her sisters.

Brigid smiled. "Go, both of you." She hugged them.

"Keep them safe," she heard her husband whisper.

"I will," she grinned, "I can't tell you what a

relief it is that you know about our magic. My sisters will be so excited to practice their wand skills."

"Brigid, did your grandmother explain how magic can be traced? I am begging you not to use your magic outside the confines of this house."

"I'll be right back," Belenos said as he took out his wand, heading out of their French doors.

"Mother." Brigid flicked her wand over her outstretched palm. Four ancient books Artemis recognized from her childhood appeared. "Grandma and Grandpa left these with us to understand our magic and history."

A smile curved her lips. "Yes, they will give you the basics. You all will need formal training." She brushed a lock of hair out of her daughter's eyes. "Your father and I might have made a mistake keeping this from all of you. We wanted you all to have an ordinary life and let you decide for yourself if you wanted to be part of this world and everything it entails." Artemis held Brigid's stare. "Your father believes the Cathain boys are warlocks and are up to something. So I mean it, please, don't leave this house or open the shop." She hugged Brigid again.

"I promise, Mother, we won't leave the grounds."

"Are you ready, my love?" Her husband held

out his hand from the balcony.

The small bag floated over with a wave of her hand, and she clasped it closed. "Tell your sisters we are sorry and love them to the moon and back." A tear slipped down her cheek as she took Belenos's hand. "Be careful."

"Be the leader you were born to be, our child," Belenos said before Brigid vanished from their view as they disappeared.

CHAPTER 3

Before they vanished, Brigid stared at the spot outside the French doors where her parents stood. Someday they would teach her and her sisters how to disappear into thin air. But, now, Brigid had mixed emotions, excited they could practice magic out in the open and scared about keeping her sisters safe from the threat their grandparents were involved in, which she didn't understand. The one risk she did understand came from Erebos. He liked her and seemed fascinated by all of her sisters. But her skin gave a creepy crawling feeling every time he looked at them, especially Aradia.

She made sure the doors were locked and made her way down the hall to her and Demeter's room.

"They're gone?" Demeter asked from behind her as she walked in.

Brigid jumped, placing a hand over her heart to keep it in her chest. "Goddesses! You know how much I hate when you sneak up on me."

"I woke up with a strange eerie feeling like something terrible happened. Then I looked over and saw you were gone."

She wrapped an arm around Demeter's shoulder, walking them back to her bed. "Something..."

"What's going on, and where are Mom and Dad?" Cassandra pointed her wand at them, keeping Aradia behind her.

"So everyone is up." Brigid motioned them in. She flicked her wrist as they crossed the threshold, and the door closed.

"I had a vision Mom and Dad left us," Cassandra said as Aradia sat next to Demeter.

"Come." She held out her hand for Cassandra to hold and sit next to her. "Yes. Mom and Dad went to help Grandma and Grandpa."

Aradia started to wring her fingers. "When will they be back?"

Demeter pulled Aradia close to her as they all looked over expectantly at Brigid. "I honestly don't know. They will keep us informed. In the meantime, we are not to leave or open the shop." She held each one of their stares. "Email all of your professors in the morning, letting them know we had a family emergency."

"I did a special candle order for Sarah to pick up today. You know how long she and George have been trying to conceive," Demeter reminded her.

"Maybe you could call her to pick it up from the back door," Brigid offered.

Demeter nodded. "I will. Is there anything else we should prepare for?"

"I'm not sure. I know we need to do more research on Ville de Cougar."

"Those are just stories." Cassandra shook her head.

"No, they're not." Brigid glanced at her sister. "Cassandra, have you had any other visions? You need to tell us immediately, no matter how insignificant you think it is."

"Right now, they are fragments of images with an earthquake." She glanced down. "I'm not sure what it means."

"It's okay. We will figure it out." Brigid stood up. "For now, I think we should stay together. Let's all sleep in Mom and Dad's room as we did as kids."

"At least we don't have to sleep on the floor."

Demeter hoisted Aradia up. "You can sleep in between Brigid and me if you like."

Aradia nodded. "Cassandra and I can sleep between you both."

Brigid led the way back to their parent's room with a smile. Once everyone was settled, she waved her wand as one of her parents' spell books hovered at the end of the bed where she stood. She flipped through the pages to find a more potent concealment charm.

"You know spells are stronger if more than one witch casts them."

With a start, she juggled the book. "Goddesses! Demeter," Brigid hissed, securing the book in both hands. She turned to see her sisters standing behind her with their wands out.

"If we all cast the spell, it will be four times as strong, and we can all sleep." Aradia came forward to help hold the gold book open.

Brigid flipped through the pages. "Here, this one will seal the room."

They all studied the words and then spoke with two wands pointed at the French doors and the bedroom entrance. "Goddess of the Moon and Star's Con-ceal-guardium asaftous."

"Will this help you all sleep?" Brigid closed the

book, walking to the bed.

Nodding, her sisters followed. Lowering the lights, Brigid kept watching until her sisters fell asleep. Then, finally, she reached under her pillow for her wand and flicked it. On her lap appeared the book of Ville de Cougar. "The more research you do, the better you understand. The more you empower yourself," she whispered her grandmother's words.

Brigid woke up in the morning to Cassandra and Aradia whispering to each other.

"You both know the end of the bed is open to get out." Demeter yawned.

"We didn't want to wake Brigid," Cassandra sighed. "Because she was up half the night reading."

"I know," Demeter replied, getting out of bed with a stretch. "Who wants to try making breakfast?"

The younger two scrambled out of bed. "Without magic," Brigid added and chuckled at how her sisters halted with a collective sigh. "Bring down your computers so we can send out the emails."

With a flick of her wand, she unsealed the door. Instead of making eggs, the girls grabbed bowls and a cereal box. Brigid made them all some of their father's strong tea. "After you finish sending your emails, we need to pack for an emergency," Brigid said, getting up and going to the sink to wash out her bowl. "Demeter, did you get a hold of Sarah to pick up the candle?"

"Yes, she will come to pick it up after George leaves for work at the hospital," her sister replied, handing Brigid her bowl.

"So what time will that be?" She started washing the other dish. "Cassandra, can you please gather all of our backpacks?"

"I think Sarah said after two-thirty," Demeter answered, taking the dishtowel to dry the dishes.

Brigid watched her younger sisters head for the door. "Aradia, remember to keep the lights out in the shop if you are heading that way."

Aradia turned. "Can't Demeter put a charm on the glass windows?"

"No magic outside Mom and Dad's room," she reminded her. "So Cassandra, bring the backpacks to their room so we can place a charm on them. Aradia, grab what you think we will need from the workshop."

"I will help you, Aradia." Demeter tossed the dishrag on the counter. "I think we should grab the healing crystals and the herbs."

"I agree. Let's meet upstairs in a half hour. It will give me time to finish up in the kitchen."

They all gathered in front of their parents' bed.

Brigid and her sisters searched the spell book and found the 'store infinite' charm. Once the spell was placed on each bag, the girls went about packing.

Most of the rest of the morning and afternoon they spent packing. Brigid shook her head at her sisters' strange choices packed for the trip. But then, she hoped they didn't have to take the journey.

"Demeter, it's getting close to two-thirty. Maybe you should put the candle out for Sarah," Brigid pointed out, gathering her schoolbooks.

"Aradia, can you go with her and grab my tarot cards?" Cassandra asked, putting some sweaters in her bag.

"Sure," Aradia answered as she folded the multi-colored blanket at the end of the bed.

Cassandra came around the bed and walked over to the desk in front of the window. "Do you think we should leave a note for Mom and Dad in case we have to leave?"

"This is why you were valedictorian." Brigid sat down and pulled out some paper. "What should we say?"

"We should keep it cryptic, something only Mom and Dad would understand."

"Perfect." Brigid started to write the note. *Follow the real story*, she wrote.

A gasp came from behind her, and Cassandra grabbed her head then fell to the floor. "Aradia!" she screamed.

Brigid ran to her. "What do you see?"

Cassandra forced herself up, running for the door, "He's going to get her!"

"Who going to get who?" Brigid followed her sister downstairs.

They charged into the workshop, where Aradia was doubled over in pain at the open back door holding Sarah's hand.

"What happened, and why is the door open?" Brigid shouted as Cassandra rushed over to her sisters, huddled on the floor.

"Sarah came early and hugged Aradia, thanking her for the candle," Demeter answered, whispering words in Aradia's ear as her head rested on Demeter's lap.

Sarah remained next to her. "I just wanted to thank her. But when she was touching me, all my pain went away."

Brigid gently separated their joined hands. "Sarah." She held her stare and concentrated as her sister moaned. "We hope the candle helps. Go home and prepare for a beautiful night with George."

They watched Sarah get up mechanically, leave,

and then focused on their withering sister.

"Aradia, what is happening?" Cassandra ran her hands up and down Aradia's body.

"Pain in my back and stomach, breaking in two." Aradia curled into a ball, panting.

Brigid put her arm under her sister's shoulders. "Let's try and get her up and bring her to Mom and Dad's room.

"I'll help her." Erebos stood at the door. His dark hair was wild and sticking up around his pale, dirt-smudged face. He pulled Aradia up by her arm as she screamed.

"Erebos." Brigid pulled out her wand, pointing at him. "What are you doing here? Let my sister go!"

He dragged Aradia outside into the pouring rain. Brigid and her sisters ran after them. Erebos held a scared, bewildered Aradia against the front of his body so they all could not get an excellent shot to curse him. "I'm sorry," he shouted, "but I have to do this. It's the only way. She is coming, and we will use her until she dies."

Brigid shook as she willed her terrified emotions down and focused on the earth to bring it up. "Please, Erebos, you don't have to do this." The ground shook under their feet; a large crack formed in the asphalt, getting wider as it went towards

Aradia and Erebos.

"I'm sorry." He turned to her sister and said something she couldn't hear over the ground rumbling.

Demeter and Cassandra jumped back to the building as the earth opened up. Erebos lost his grip on her sister. Brigid ran, leaping over the large opening, grasping Aradia by the arm as the world parted further and Erebos disappeared. "Got you!" she shouted over the loud rumble of the huge boulders falling into the gaping hole in the alley. Brigid secured Aradia to her chest and ran to the shop's open door. "Close the door, Demeter, and seal all the entrances with Cassandra."

Aradia collapsed on the floor. "You saved me." She heaved out a heavy breath.

"Of course, I will always come for you." Brigid knelt beside her sister. "Are you alright? Did Erebos hurt you?"

"No. Erebos seemed distracted before the ground opened. He was trying to..."

Demeter rushed over and pulled Aradia up. "We have to go. Cassandra says we are still in danger."

"I'll grab the books and place a note in their place." Brigid stood and checked all the entrances were secure. Chaos met her in their parents' room.

Everyone but Aradia grabbed their bag and began throwing more things into them. Brigid glanced at her sister lying on the bed and wondered if she could continue their escape. She took the note off the desk and raced to the library to the secret cabinet. Before sealing the door, she placed the books in her backpack and left the message.

They met in the hallway. "Cassandra, which entrance is safe for us to go out?" Demeter asked while holding up Aradia between them.

"The roof." Cassandra motioned to the attic stairs. "We will have to use our brooms." She summoned them all.

Brigid raised her sister's pale face. Demeter held her up. "Aradia, do you think you can fly?" Her head flopped back and forth. "I will take her on my broom."

Once on the roof, Cassandra and Demeter helped secure Aradia on Brigid's broom. She whispered through the pouring rain, "We need to use the cloaking charm so no one sees us."

Demeter waved her wand over all of them. "Conceal."

"Which way?" Cassandra asked as they took off.

"Southeast," Brigid pointed as Aradia wavered. "Demeter, take the lead to the border."

They flew through the gray skies shivering from the cold. Brigid wanted to do another spell to keep them dry and warm but knew it would leave a trace. So she held her sister tighter. "I'm sorry, sweetie, once we get out of this storm and land, we can change."

Checking again to see if they were followed, Brigid wondered how she would find Ville de Cougar and keep her sisters safe. "Goddesses of the earth and sky, please help us." As the soft plea left her lips, the rain stopped. A streak of colors broke through the clouds. She noticed it ended on the horizon in a forest as she followed it. "Follow the rainbow!" she called to her sisters.

Demeter came up beside her. "You're quoting the Lucky Charms guy?"

A smile curved her lips. "No, I think the Goddesses are leading our way."

"Let's hope they lead us to safety, not a pot of gold."

"We have to trust the fates," she murmured, then pondered what the fates had in store for them.

Katrina A. Bauer

About the Author

Katrina A. Bauer lives in a sweet little suburb of Chicago with her husband, who fills her life with laughter every day (usually at his own expense) and obsesses over how her four sassy daughters navigate adulting. When not writing contemporary and paranormal romance, she tries to avoid a clingy chocolate lab while reading romance, drinking tea, and savoring pieces of chocolate, which she also rewards herself with after writing a great scene.

To learn more about her upcoming books, giveaways, and events, you can sign up for Kat's newsletter on her website:

www.katrinaabauer.com

www.facebook.com/KatrinaABauerAuthor
www.instagram.com/katrinaabauer
www.twitter.com/katrinaabauer
www.pinterest.com/katrinaabauer

The Hot Hearts Café Series

Want to read more from the Hot Hearts Café series?

My Cinnamon Roll by Lia Violet
Life's Sweeter on Land by Ginger Leone

Cougartown & Hot Hearts Café
Bearly Festive by Lia Violet
Magical Holiday Fruitcake Rolls by Trinity Blacio
Raffle of the Heart by Trinity Blacio

Flames Of Light series
Bound by Flames by Katrina A. Bauer

www.ingramcontent.com/pod-product-compliance
Lightning Source LLC
Chambersburg PA
CBHW070811120626
46557CB00002B/806